# On a Starry Night

A MELANIE KROUPA BOOK

# On a Starry Night

*by* Natalie Kinsey-Warnock

*illustrations by* David McPhail

Orchard Books   New York

*To my brother, Leland — N.K.W.*

*For Dorothy, fellow painter and charming niece — D.M.*

Library of Congress Cataloging-in-Publication Data

Kinsey-Warnock, Natalie.

On a starry night / by Natalie Kinsey-Warnock ; illustrations by David McPhail.

p.  cm.

"A Melanie Kroupa book" — Half t.p.

Summary: On a starry night a girl and her mother climb the hill above their farm, watching and listening to the natural world around them.

ISBN 0-531-06820-X. — ISBN 0-531-08670-4 ( lib. bdg. )

[1. Nature — Fiction. 2. Night — Fiction. 3. Mothers and daughters — Fiction.] I. McPhail, David M., ill. II. Title.

PZ7.K62930n 1994

[E]—dc20                                                                    93-4878

Orchard Books

95 Madison Avenue

New York, NY 10016

Manufactured in the United States of America

Printed by Barton Press, Inc.

Bound by Horowitz/Rae

10 9 8 7 6 5 4 3 2 1

The text of this book is set in 16 pt. Goudy. The illustrations are acrylic on paper.

On a starry night,
Mama and I climb the hill
where nighthawks swoop
and the dark woods rattle with crickets and frogs.

Far below us,
where our farm sits in the valley,
a few lights twinkle from the barn
where Papa is milking.
I hear Shep barking,
and the jingle of cowbells.

When Mama and I come here
on bright summer days,
I race ahead to look for wild strawberries,
and daisies for Mama to braid in my hair.
But when we come to watch stars,
I hold on tight to Mama's hand.

The night noises follow us
and I look over my shoulder
for the things that hide behind dark trees.

Sometimes we see deer
on the edges of the field at twilight,
and sometimes we see raccoons
all lined up in a row,
their eyes as bright as beads.

We lay our blankets
where deer have lain and flattened the grass
to make a bed just for us, it seems.
I close my eyes and smell spruce trees,
sharp and spicy like the spruce gum
Papa brings home from the woods.

Somewhere off in those trees,
a  barred owl hoots,
hoohoo-hoohoo, hoohoo-hoohooaw,
and something nearer snuffles and snorts,
something like a big black bear, I think,
looking for his supper.

I snuggle closer to Mama,
but she says he's looking for beechnuts
or a tree where bees have stored honey,
and he won't bother us.
Mama never seems afraid of anything.

Sometimes coyotes come spilling over the hill like a waterfall,
yapping and yeowling a wild coyote song.
Sometimes we hear foxes, and some nights we don't.
That's part of the magic, Mama says.
You never know what you'll see, or smell, or hear.

All around us,
fireflies blink and flicker like sparks
up into the sky
until I can't tell them from the stars.

I find the Big Dipper
and the Great Bear who prowls the northern sky.
Mama points out Pegasus the Winged Horse
and Cygnus the Swan.
The stars look close enough to touch.

"I used to be afraid of the dark," Mama says,
"even when I was older than you,
until my father, your grandfather,
took me out to watch stars.
We heard owls, and saw the northern lights,
like brightly colored scarves, dance across the sky,
and I forgot to be afraid."

All of a sudden a branch snaps,
and something large and dark
swishes through the grass.
"Where's my girl?" Papa sings out.
He's come from the barn, the milking done.
I jump up and hug his knees.
"Right here, Papa!"

Papa laughs and swings me up into the air,
up into the black night.
I am a nighthawk soaring on the wind,
but I am flying higher than any nighthawk,
higher, higher —
up toward the Great Bear!
His sharp teeth glitter like ice.

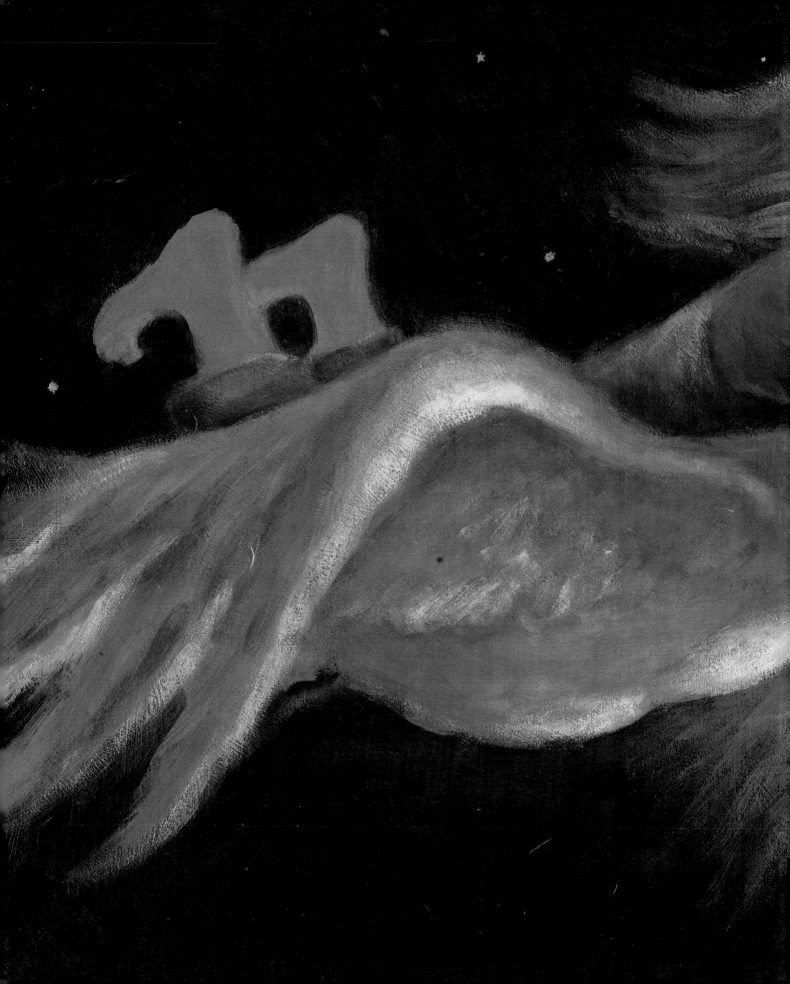

Just in time the Swan scoops me up.
I feel the whoosh of wind
and the powerful beat of wings.

He sets me on Pegasus' strong back.
I grab his mane
and we sail across the sky.

Stars and planets spin by us
like ribbon from a spool.
I want to fly forever —
past Jupiter's moons
and Saturn's rings
and back along the Milky Way.

I hear the whisper of stars
and pounding hooves
like a heart beating
and then I fall, fall,
back into Papa's arms.

Mama, Papa, and I
lie on our blankets and count shooting stars

Then Papa carries me home.
I say good-bye to the crickets and frogs
and the twinkling stars.

Next time,
I'll bring an apple for Pegasus
and a ribbon for his mane
and I won't be afraid at all.